DUCKS RUN AMOK!

To Lynda—JEM

PENGUIN WORKSHOP
An Imprint of Penguin Random House LLC, New York

Copyright © 2021 by Jennifer Morris. All rights reserved.
Published simultaneously in hardcover and paperback by Penguin Workshop, an imprint of Penguin Random House LLC, New York. PENGUIN and PENGUIN WORKSHOP are trademarks of Penguin Books Ltd, and the W colophon is a registered trademark of Penguin Random House LLC.
Manufactured in China.

Visit us online at www.penguinrandomhouse.com.

Library of Congress Cataloging-in-Publication Data is available upon request.

ISBN 9780593222911 (hc)   10 9 8 7 6 5 4 3 2 1

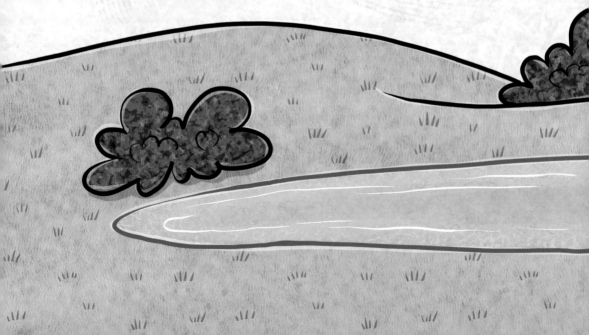

DUCKS RUN AMOK!

by J. E. Morris

Penguin Workshop

A flock of ducks
flies in a row.
They look and see
a pond below.

They stop their flight
to take a swim.
Soon the pond's
full to the brim.

The ducks all flap.
They splish and splash.
A party starts,
a poolside bash.

Some more ducks come
and join the crowd.

A duck band plays.
They're really loud.

All kinds of ducks
are on the scene.
Old ducks, young ducks,
even green.

Some ducks have flat webby toes.

Green duck has a stubby nose.

Green duck's back
is hard and tough.
He has no down.
He has no fluff.

But ducks don't look
at shell or feather.
Ducks are ducks—
they flock together.

The ducks all dance.
They spin and quack.

Their tummies growl—
they need a snack.

Hey look! Some ducks
inside a truck
are selling pies
and cakes. What luck!

The ducks like cakes
and all the rest,
but they like sweet
cream pies the best.

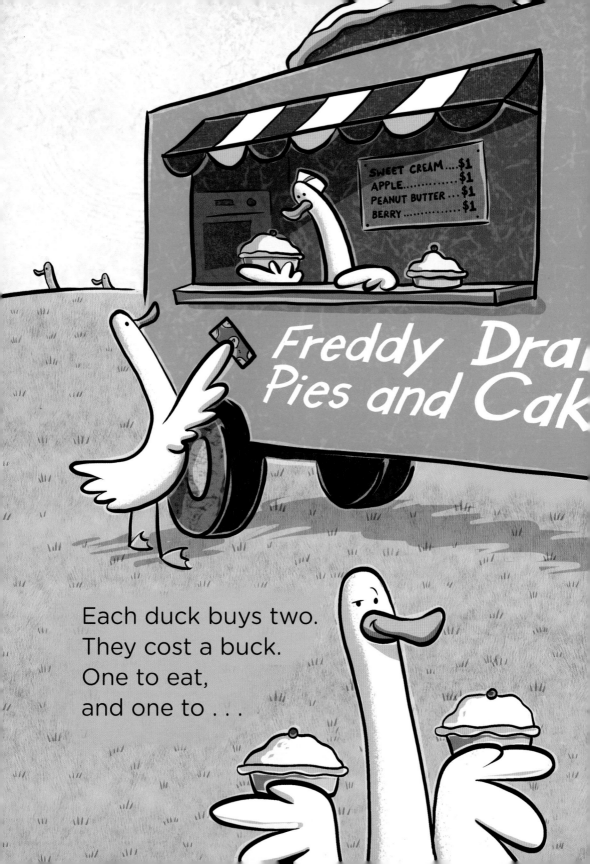

SWEET CREAM....$1
APPLE..............$1
PEANUT BUTTER...$1
BERRY..............$1

Freddy Dra
Pies and Cak

Each duck buys two.
They cost a buck.
One to eat,
and one to . . .

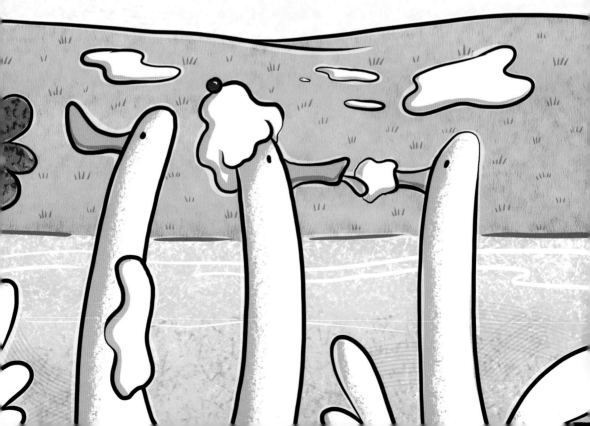

The pie ducks hop
into their truck.
The rest clean up
the sticky muck.

The flock heads off
to parts unknown.

The green duck stays
there all alone.